For Christy Hawkins

First U.S. edition 2009

Library of Congress Cataloging-in-Publication Data is available.
Library of Congress Catalog Card Number 2008933310

ISBN 978-0-7636-4273-0

2 4 6 8 10 9 7 5 3 1

Printed in China

This book was typeset in MT Schoolbook.
The illustrations were done in mixed media.

Candlewick Press
99 Dover Street
Somerville, Massachusetts 02144

visit us at www.candlewick.com

Tilly and
her friends
all live
together in
a little yellow
house. . . .

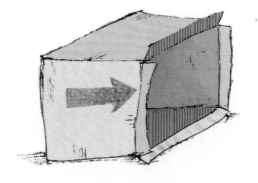

Where's Tumpty?

Polly Dunbar

Candlewick Press

Tumpty
had his eyes
closed.

Tightly closed.

"Hello, Tumpty,"
said Tilly.
"What are you
doing?"

"I'm hiding," Tumpty said.

"You can't see me."

But Tilly **could** see Tumpty.

So Tumpty tried hiding
under a large cardboard box
with his eyes tightly closed.

"What is
Tumpty doing?"
asked
Hector.

"He's
hiding!"
said Tilly.

"But I can see him," laughed Hector.

So Tumpty tried hiding behind a plant,
under a large cardboard box,
with his eyes tightly closed.

"What is Tumpty up to?" asked Pru.

"He's hiding," said Hector.

"Don't be silly," said Pru. "I can see him."

So Tumpty tried hiding upside down, behind
a plant, under a large cardboard box,
with his eyes tightly closed.

"Ha, ha, ha!"
laughed Doodle.
"Look at Tumpty."

"He's hiding," said Pru.

"Humpf," said Tumpty.

"Tumpty is so
funny,"
said
Tiptoe.

Everybody
laughed and laughed.

They

laughed

and

laughed

and  laughed.

"Hang on,"
said Doodle.
"Where's
Tumpty?"

"He must
be hiding,"
Hector
said.

"Let's look
for him,"
said
Tilly.

"Are you in here?"
asked Tilly,
looking in
the cupboard.

Tumpty wasn't there.

"I bet he's behind the curtains!" said Hector.

Tumpty wasn't there.

"Nope,
he's not here either,"
said Doodle,
looking under the table.

"Perhaps
he's in
the cookie jar,"
said
Tiptoe.

Tumpty definitely wasn't
there, but there were
some **cookies**.

"I miss Tumpty," said Doodle.

"Perhaps he's really gone," said Tiptoe.

"Forever!" cried Hector.

"I'm here!" trumpeted Tumpty,
jumping out from behind the sofa.

"I was only hiding!"

"Hurrah! We love

you, Tumpty!" said everyone.

"You're so good at hiding," said Tilly.

"I know," said Tumpty, and he finished off all the cookies.

The End